HORROR
BEFORE IT WAS
COOL

Horror
Before It Was Cool

A Hipster Horror Anthology

Edited by Jonathan W. Thurston

Horror Before It Was Cool

Edited by Jonathan W. Thurston

Weasel Press

Manvel, TX

http://www.weaselpress.com

CONTENTS

Introduction
Thurston Howl

Welcome to the first volume of the Before It Was Cool series! As a self-proclaimed hipster myself, I kept finding myself returning to a discourse in my writing community: what would hipster noir look like? We imagined coffee instead of booze, meeting at a café instead of a bar, taking an Uber instead of a taxi, and gay sex as opposed to the heteronormative "damsel in distress." In that conversation, I tried reimagining other genres in a hipster world: fantasy, sci fi, Westerns, etc. That spawned this series. I wanted to start with horror since that was my personal specialty. I asked writers to re-envision horror tropes through a hipster lens, and the results are astounding.

Some writers here take a parodic approach, taking popular horror narratives and making them comically hipster. Some take a more serious approach, showing how horrific a world could be with a hipster flair. Some even show being hipster to be the horror itself. The writers produced short stories, flash fiction, and poetry. And the mix of representation is great with these authors, too, and I do like diversity.

So, regardless of if you're coming here as a hipster, as a horror fanatic, or just as someone looking for a hella good book to read, you're in the right place. Take a puff of your vaping device, grab a cup of our organic coffee, and sit back in our locally made armchairs. And don't worry about the blood splatters that might hit you: they were all humanely killed. You can trust us.

DEAD GIRL BLUES
KARI ANN EBERT

You come over every night like clockwork.

No. More like bloodwork.

I know it disgusts you, makes you queasy. Still you come and knock your angry knock.

I can hear your slow breathing through the door. You say it helps you stay conscious. Learned it after the knitting circle *she* made you go to one night, and then some yoga broke out.

Pranayama practice. Now it's your go-to. When the dizziness overwhelms you like a wave, you breathe.

You must be dizzy tonight. *On the verge of being overwhelmed*, I think as I press my ear against the cold door.

I used to wonder how you could do it, but not tonight. Tonight, I'm numb. I try to remember how it felt at the beginning.

You knock again. Angrier.

I like to wait until I think you'll break. It's good for you.

My chest flutters. A ghost of the former thrill.

You slam the door wide when I finally unbolt it. You're not here for games.

I watch you spread the shower curtain on the floor. 101 Dalmatians. You saved it from the trash when you were an avid freegan.

Too much effort, you'd said after a week or two. *I'll just shoot for zero waste.*

You sit on the bed. Legs wide. Trench coat still on. Black non-vegan boots on the edge of plastic. It's ok. They're second-hand, so you're honoring the animal's death.

I shut the door. Deadbolt it. I can almost hear the rage in your veins grinding faster and faster. I walk in stocking feet as slowly as I can. Hear the whisper of silk as my thighs rub against each other.

You'll have none of that. You point to the floor in front of you.

"Down," you say.

It will be the only word spoken, bouncing off my empty walls and shelves.

I step onto the shower curtain. Turn my back to you. Kneel.

I know not to unbutton my dress. Leave my black hair loose down my back. These are the two pleasures that are yours and yours alone.

The first time I'd worn the Gunne Sax dress I found in my Aunt's attic, you thought I was mocking you. So many little buttons from nape of neck to small of back.

No, I'd said, *I thought you'd enjoy slowing it down.*

I hear your breath catch. You start with the top button— tenderly loosen each one. My chest vibrates. You've gotten quicker at handling the tiny pearls and toggles over time.

You yank the dress down over my arms. I know not to move. You stroke my hair, sweep it aside exposing my bare back and neck. You stroke it again, a little slower.

Then, pause.

I hear you smelling your hand. Wonder if you like my new vanilla-ginger shampoo.

Only things that smell like food, you told me once.

Pleasure over, we're back to business. You snap your fingers. I bow my head. Place my hands on my knees.

This makes the skin on my back taut. You don't like the way it feels when the blade goes through. Stretching makes it quicker.

I hear you get everything ready. Thick plastic unrolled from your coat pocket. The sing of the blade being unsheathed. I used to joke that it sounded like a mini samurai sword (when we still talked).

½ pint every day is still dangerous, you'd said. *But it's the bare minimum she needs to survive.*

You never say her name.

I feel your warm fingers moving down the rows of old scars. My skin is cold, like a museum.

You take a deep breath. I know to dig my nails into my knees.

It doesn't hurt anymore, but I can't let you know. You already have one dead girl. You don't need two.

I let out a counterfeit groan as you slice into the skin. There's a gurgle, then you catch the red liquid flowing like a faucet. The bag you swiped from the clinic has seen better days, but it still does the job.

The gurgle wasn't blood. I know this.

You're trying to hold your lunch down until the bag is filled, sealed, and you've taped cotton gauze over my wound. You stopped eating dinner in hopes of curbing the nausea. But no length of time is enough. You always revisit your meals.

You made it this time. Finished the job. Other times you weren't so lucky: we were left with a mess. And *she* was left with her hunger.

I hold steady, feel the throb in my back. I can hear you in the bathroom.

I wonder what you had for lunch. Khachapuri or a poké bowl? Neither of which we've ever shared. It used to be pizza delivery after we were done. Now it's not even that.

I stay kneeling with my dress down around my arms, and pulled up past my thighs. I feel one garter strap that's come undone, dangling free. I leave it there. Keep pressing my nails into my knees. You never miss the little details, and I still want you to find pleasure somehow. This is the only thing physical between us now.

I'm dizzy. The daily reaping takes its toll. I grab the nightstand to steady myself. Then quickly put my hand back on my knee.

I read you should only give blood once a month, I said once.

You quickly changed the subject. I let you.

You come out of the bathroom. The light engulfs your head. Makes you look like a saint. I expect you to bless me as you place your hand on my head.

You stroke my hair, lift my dress back onto my shoulders. Reattach the wayward garter, let your hand brush the silk of my stocking.

I stand up as you put the bag of crimson liquid into your pocket. I'm dwarfed by your height.

Anger sated, you take my hand. Then drop it and leave. No words.

The door stands open. I consider leaving it that way. The distance seems too much to travel, but I manage. Holding onto furniture along the way.

Iron-rich foods, you'd told me. *Eat steak and spinach afterwards.* But cereal is easier when you have no strength.

I sit down at the table I set before you came. The original Count Chocula I found online. Bowl. Spoon. Milk. My own private joke.

If you noticed, you never mention it.

The rest of my night is spent thinking of *her*. The other dead girl.

Does she know where you get it from? Do you watch her drink it? Do you run to the bathroom and heave, or is that weakness only reserved for me?

I try not to let one final question surface, though I know it's inevitable. It's the only one I know the real answer to.

I finish the cereal and walk to the bed.

I leave the bowl on the table. Shower curtain on the floor. I'll clean in the morning, though I feel weaker each day.

I slip out of the dress. Leave it lying where it lands. When my head hits the pillow, the question overwhelms me like an unstoppable flood. Red and warm and thick.

If it were the other way around, would you do the same for me?

CHUTH-WHO-LU
BEULAH VEGA

The packed, warm brewpub grew silent as the host climbed onstage. The guest band stopped tuning and looked out at the large audience.

"Ladies and gentlemen and all those in-between," the host began, his deep voice booming in what seemed like the pit of the guitarist's stomach, "we here at the bearded chicken brewhouse are so glad that you could join us for the release of our new Elder ale."

The band looked at each other, as the crowd clapped appreciatively.

"What's an Elder ale?" the bassist mouthed to the drummer.

"I don't know," the drummer signed back at him.

But the host was not paying attention to them.

The host, a tall man with curly black hair, and a salt-and-pepper beard trimmed in such a way to give a sharp edge to an otherwise aging jawline, rolled up his shirtsleeves to reveal a tattoo of an anchor on one brawny forearm, and the tattoo of a cephalopod doing something obscene on the other. "Before the grand unveiling though" the host continued, "I would like to introduce our guest artists for the ceremony, please welcome to the stage the Atari 64's!"

So saying, he turned from the mic to the band and gestured with fingers that seemed a little longer than they should have been.

The guitarist shot a worried look to the lead singer, who just shook his head. They had received weirder introductions, and this gig paid well. Besides, the crowd had roared at their introduction, and he was loath to disappoint an audience.

As they launched into their opening song (a pop/grunge

cover of "Raindrops Keep Falling on My Head"), the bassist saw the host take a shiny pocket watch out of the brocade vest he was wearing.

The host looked up and stared straight into the bassist's eyes. But there was something very wrong with the host's eyes: they had grown huge and black, where before they had been a soft grey-green and of the usual size. The bassist was so taken aback that he missed the next two notes, and the guitarists not so casually walked across the stage to kick him in the shin, under the guise of changing a level on the amp.

Brought back to the task at hand, the bassist decided that perhaps his eyes had played tricks on him, and by the time they had launched into their prog/metal cover of "Come on, Eileen," he had gotten back into his groove.

Finally, the first half of the set was over, and the band took a much-needed break. The green room in the brew-pub was small but clean, and the host had provided them with delicious-looking vegan delicacies as well as a pony keg of the pub's signature beer the I.P. Egg.

Their manager/merch-seller/girlfriend of the lead singer was waiting for them with bottles of water as well as towels for band members like the drummer who exerted so much more energy on stage.

As they settled in for their 15-minute break she asked them "Did you guys notice anything odd about the audience?"

"There are a lot of kids for a brew-pub," the bassist said.

"Well, yeah, there's that, but this place does have a reputation for being really family-friendly. But," she continued, "don't you think they all kind of look alike?"

The guitarist laughed. "Don't all hipsters kind of look alike?"

His bandmates joined in the laughter, and the manager/merch-seller/girlfriend had to agree.

The lead singer took the lull after the laughter to ask if anyone thought it would be a big deal if he had a beer before they went back on stage.

The band agreed that not only was it not a big deal, but that they should all join him for the sake of playing consistently with each other.

"This doesn't taste the way I remember," the drummer, who was a known micro-brew snob said.

"It tastes fine to me," the guitarist replied.

"Let me try," the manager/merch-seller/girlfriend asked.

"It tastes good," the drummer went on as if the others had not spoken. "Just the right amount of hops, low bitterness with some salty/caramel undertones. I just seem to remember the I.P. Egg having a more robust flavor the last time I had it."

"Probably because this is a pony keg, and you had it bottled," the lead singer said sagely. "We all know you can't really say you've tasted a microbrew unless you've tasted it on tap."

The other band members nodded their heads at this wisdom as they finished their glasses, right as the host knocked on the door to let them know that the fifteen minutes was almost up.

Having used the relevant facilities, the band clambered back onstage as the manager/merch-seller/girlfriend took her place at the back of the room behind the merch table.

It was probably the drummer who noticed the change first. His hands seemed to start drumming on their own. He had always prided himself on being a good drummer, but he had never been truly great. Now he was phenomenal. The bassist was next, then the guitarist, last the raspy voice of the lead singer cleared, and he was suddenly singing in the same key the band was playing. The crowd was going crazy.

But the drummer then realized that he didn't know what he was playing. The rhythm was unlike anything he had played before. The bassist soon joined, and then the guitarist started playing a melody unlike anything the band had heard; it was almost as if the instruments themselves were singing in some unknowable, unfathomable language, and the band members were the instruments. The lead soon found himself saying words that he could not understand. His tongue and jaw hurt from pronouncing syllables that should not go together, his throat was getting hoarse from the guttural language it seemed to be producing all on its own. He looked up at the crowd, scanning for his girlfriend, but she was not at her station. He realized then that she was standing beside him, singing harmony to the strange ill-tasting words. He had no idea how long she had been there, but her lips were starting to bleed from the contortions necessary to make the sounds come from her slim body.

The lead looked around the room now and not a single scrap of flannel was left in the crowd. No elaborate mustaches, no funny-colored vans or gauged earrings. Now the crowd. Men and women wore hoods, deep and black, and he swore that when he looked into the hoods their eyes had grown huge, round, and black, like dolls' eyes.

He scanned the room for the children that had been there, but what he saw instead were little hunched things, with hairy backs and pointed claws, Hobbes, he knew without knowing how they've turned into Hobgoblins. As this revelation hit, his vision started to dim, and a great roar filled his ears: something had entered the brew-pub, something that now filled the large open barrel house behind him. Something that caused the black-robed inhuman audience to fall to their knees. He could not turn to look, as the chanting words held him bound in place, but he heard the drummer cry out as the drums stopped, he heard the bass hit the floor and then a second later the guitar, and he saw out of the corner of his eye as a long tendril of flesh, or scale, or skin, or something wrapped around his manager/merch-seller/ girlfriend and pulled her back so hard, her false eyelashes fell off onto the stage.

He knew what was coming, but he had no recourse as the lithe tentacle-like object wrapped around his waist, and as he was flung back toward the brewing vat, he saw the host let go of him, and he saw the large black mass holding the brewing vat like a pint jar.

My Curious Dog
James B. Nicola

My dog barks once a year into a corner
at someone, some *thing*, only he can see—
a soul seeking remembrance—or a mourner—
with a frightening fury, and relentlessly.
Last year when he went crazy there, I thought
it must have been the crankling of the heat
in the pipes. But they calmed down, while he did not,
so maybe I was wrong. And he's the sweet-
est dog! What happened there to make him bite
the air and growl in such a ghastly way
for hours until the wee hours of the night,
when his sweet self returned?
                                        Yesterday
the heat was off, and Fido's frenzy filled
the house, again, inscrutably, with fear.
If I recall, though, last year I penciled
in, on the kitchen calendar, *when* he
started and stopped. Here's the page—precisely
the same times—to the minute—as this year.

James and Jackie
John Power

"Is that a bear claw?" James asked, as Tom was about to take a bite of his breakfast.

"Yeah"

"That doesn't really look like an actual bear claw."

"Bears aren't pastry," Tom countered.

"Why'd they name it a bear claw anyway? Who wants to eat a bear's claw?"

"A pastry bear or an actual bear?"

"An actual bear. It's like eating pigs feet."

"People eat pigs' feet."

"Not pastry pigs' feet."

"What's a pastry pig?"

"I'd imagine something like a pastry bear, only more pig-like and less bear-like."

"That would make sense."

"Really, think about it, who wants to be eating a disgusting furry bloody foot with claws on it?"

"No one. That's why it's made of pastry. What about your cruller?" Tom accused.

"Crullers don't claim to be a bear's claw."

"Considering crullers can't speak."

"That's part of it."

"This conversation is going nowhere," noticed Tom.

"Well, it's going somewhere; it's just going to very a bad place," James responded.

The two chuckled as they sat in their coffee shop on Prince Street on Friday morning, and then looked at their papers folded on the table. Tom took a bite of his bear claw and opened his paper to the local news section, and started reading about police brutality. James sipped his coffee and looked at the sports. The Jets would play in Buffalo in two days. It looked to be a good game.

The former college roommates came to this coffee shop every morning. The shop was larger than it needed to be considering they were the only ones who actually sat down. There were five or six tables set up, but the chairs usually remained empty. Patrons would come in off the street, walk up to the huge wooden counter, and order their coffee. Except for that counter there was nothing really special about the shop. Black and brown linoleum floor. Big glass window that looked onto the street. Not enough lighting. A too strong aroma of brewing coffee and baking muffins. Nothing special at all about it really, but Tom and James had been coming here ever since they "discovered" it junior year at NYU. Old habits.

They sat there quietly, eating breakfast and drinking their coffee, while other residents of SoHo rushed in to buy their morning energy, and then rushed out again to the subway to meet jobs down in the financial district or up in midtown. Tom, though, was a writer, and James a freelance photographer. They had the luxury of working for themselves, and they enjoyed the fact that they could sit in a coffee shop in the morning for as long as they wanted before they had to get to work. Even then, Tom could say that he wasn't feeling "inspired" that day, and walk around the Village, or catch a subway out to Brooklyn. If James didn't have a paying job scheduled he could just as easily hang out in Washington Square reading some Kafka or Hemingway, and if he brought his camera with him he could snap a few shots and claim to be working on some new photo-book. As it was, though, Tom had a story he'd been thinking about for a few days and finally wanted to get down on paper. James wasn't going to sit in the shop alone even though he didn't have anything to do.

As they were reading their papers a redhead walked in, and James immediately looked up at her. Redheads always got him. Even though James' relationships tended to end unhappily for both parties, he came back to redheads every time. Tom noticed that James was now staring at the woman as she waited in line for a cup of coffee, and he suggested James go up and talk to her.

"No way. I just had a nasty breakup with Diane. I don't want a date right now."

Tom smiled. "Yeah you do, that's why you're staring. Go talk to her."

"Some random guy in New York goes up to a complete stranger in a coffee shop and asks her out on a date. She'll think I'm a weirdo."

"Hey, what if she's the weirdo, huh? Ever think of that possibility?"

James chuckled. "You're not helping . . . but if you insist." He got out of his seat and walked over to the redhead. She was being served now, so James just stood behind her and waited politely for her to finish her order. The employee handed her a cup of coffee and a bagel, she handed him a few dollars, waited for change, and then whirled around to rush out the door to get to work. In her haste she didn't realize James was standing directly behind her, and as she turned she bumped into him, spilling the entire cup of coffee on him. James jumped back and gave a little yelp of pain while Tom sat in the corner and began laughing hysterically.

"Oh, I'm so sorry!" said the redhead.

"That's all right. It's just a little hot," replied James as he continued to grimace in pain.

"I'll pay for the dry cleaning."

"No, that's all right; it was an accident. I was standing too close behind you anyway: it's my fault."

"No, no, I turned around too quickly. I'm sorry.

Please let my pay for the dry cleaning."

"No, really, it's OK. My name's James."

"I'm Jackie, and I'm so very sorry."

"It's all right, really. Actually I came over to talk to you."

"What?"

"See, now you think I'm some kind of strange New York psycho, but I'm not."

"Excuse me?" Jackie said with a puzzled look on her face.

"I was sitting over there," James pointed to the table, and Tom gave a little wave in reply, "and I saw you come in, and I thought you were pretty."

"Thank you," Jackie said, a bit unsure if that was the right response to make to this man now soaked in her coffee.

"I don't normally approach strangers. Don't think this is a normal thing for me to do."

"I won't."

"I came over to talk to you and see if you wanted to go out tonight. It's Friday and all, so I figured going out might be a good idea."

"I . . . don't . . . know," said Jackie, still a bit confused by the entire situation.

"Come on, you spilled coffee on me. The least you can let me do is take you out tonight. I give you my guarantee, I'm not a psycho. We'll only go to heavily populated places," James said with a grin.

". . .umm . . . well . . ."

"Just dinner. You've got to eat anyway, right? Let me buy you dinner. You spilled coffee on me; it's only fair."

"All right."

"Good," said James as he began to smile. "Do you know where Le Bastille is?"

"No."

"Ah, that's fine, that's fine. Let's meet here at . . .

what, seven . . . and we'll walk. It's only a few blocks, over on McDougal Street."

"OK," said Jackie, she too beginning to smile, and her blue eyes beginning to sparkle.

"Good."

"Well, I've got to get to work."

"What do you do?"

"I work for Merrill Lynch, down on Vescy Street."

"Interesting. I'm a photographer. Well, I'll let you go. I'll see you at seven."

"Bye."

Jackie walked out of the coffee shop, and James went back to his table and sat down with Tom, who was laughing and eating his bear claw. After they finished their breakfasts and papers they left the coffee shop and went their separate ways.

That night James was waiting outside the coffee shop when Jackie showed up. They walked together to Le Bastille, and were seated in a back corner. The waiter brought them some wine and bread and handed them menus, and went to check on other customers while they decided what they wanted.

"You know," said Jackie, "my roommate said I shouldn't be here with you tonight. She said you were probably some crazy psycho."

"Didn't I give you my guarantee?" laughed James.

"Well I'm new to the City and I didn't know what your guarantee was worth."

"Where are you from?"

"I'm from Michigan, but I was just living down in Atlanta."

"Atlanta. I could never live there. I'd have to be a Falcons fan."

"Things didn't quite work out in Atlanta, and I got a job up here, so I moved in with a friend from college who needed a roommate."

"When did you move in?"

"A few days ago."

"I figured you must be new. I'm in that coffee shop almost every morning, and I've never seen you before. I would have remembered you if you've been in there."

Jackie smiled. "Today was my first day at work. Looks like I started off right by spilling coffee on you."

"Don't worry about it, the doctor said it's just some second degree burns."

"You saw the doctor!?" questioned a shocked Jackie.

"No, no, I'm kidding," laughed James.

Jackie smiled. "You said you were a photographer. That must be exciting."

"Yeah, I guess. It can be. When everything goes exactly right, and everything falls into place, that's what I like."

"What kind of photography do you do?"

"All kinds. Usually people, but sometimes I take landscapes. To pay the bills I do portraits and weddings, but I hate that kind of work. Today, though, I had an interview with the *New York Post* for a photojournalism spot."

"Really! That's fantastic."

"That was my major at Yale, and I think I put a good portfolio together and had a good interview, so I hope I'll get the job. The interviewer said I was his favorite, but he still had some others to see, so he'd give me a call."

"Wow, that would be really great if you got that."

"It should give me enough money so I don't have to pay for meals by washing dishes," James said with a grin.

Jackie started laughing too, and the waiter came over, and they ordered their meals. They had a great time at dinner, and sat there long after dessert talking and laughing. Finally, they decided it was getting late, and that the maitre d' was eyeing them to leave, so James paid the check and they left. James walked Jackie to her apartment, which was only a few blocks away from his own, and she gave him a kiss goodnight. James asked if he could give her a call sometime, and she put her number into his phone. She smiled, and then went into the lobby of her building. It was still early for James on a Friday night, so he went back to his apartment and put on a movie.

The next day James met Tom at a pizza parlor on Bleecker Street for lunch. James told Tom that he had a great time last night, and that he would call Jackie again soon for another date. Tom gave James a copy of his story to read over, as he had since college. James would always make a few suggestions for plot twists and other improvements. Neither had much news to report to the other, so the meal was over quickly.

When they were done eating, James took his copy of the story, and walked back to his apartment. He walked by way of Jackie's building, on the off chance that he would see her, but didn't, so he went right home. When he got home he wanted to tell Jackie that he got the job at the *New York Post*, so he gave her a call. Voicemail picked up, and he left a message saying that he got the job, that he had a really nice dinner the night before, that he hoped to see her again, that he was sorry he got voicemail, and that he was wondering where she was. James really wanted to talk to her though, so he called back a few times that day to see if she was in. Each time he left one of those cute little "just letting you know I called" messages for her.

She didn't call back, so he called again a few times on Sunday, getting the answering machine each time. For some reason James began to think that something really terrible must have happened to Jackie. He had called her a number of times and she hadn't returned his calls, and all he could think of was that maybe her building burned down. Her building was only a few blocks from his, and he knew he would have heard the sirens from the fire trucks, but he just couldn't be positive. He grabbed his coat and left his apartment and walked over to Jackie's. It was fine. No sign of fire. He then thought maybe someone had gotten into her building, had robbed her, and then killed her and her roommate. He went into a building across the street from Jackie's, and walked up the dark and narrow stairway to the roof. He looked out across the street that separated the buildings, and into Jackie's apartment. He saw her. She was sitting on her couch watching television. He had called her all day Saturday and all day Sunday, and she hadn't called him back and she was just sitting there watching TV. James became furious. There were a few potted plants and some plastic chairs on the roof with him. He picked up the plants and threw them so that the clay pot would shatter and the black soil would spill out all over the roof. He started kicking the chairs trying to break them. When they wouldn't break, he picked them up and began bashing them on the asphalt roof. He threw one chair off the building—it didn't hit anyone. When James was done with his tantrum he again looked into Jackie's apartment. He watched her for a good quarter of an hour, just sitting there, watching TV. James returned to his apartment, got his camera, and went back to the roof. He sat there for another hour snapping pictures of Jackie. Then he saw it. He saw Jackie's head suddenly turn to look at her phone. He watched as Jackie buried her head in her hands and waited for the number to display. After a second Jackie picked her phone off the coffee table and began talking. She was screening her calls. James again became infuriated, and picked up another plant and threw it as far as he could across the roof. When he calmed down he grabbed his camera, snapped a few more pictures, and returned to his apartment.

Monday morning again found Tom and James in the coffee shop. James gave Tom a marked up copy of his story, and Tom read over it asking James to explain some of the comments. When that exercise was done, Tom read the paper, ate his bear claw, and went about his day like it was any other regular day. James however, was at the coffee shop for one reason. He was waiting for Jackie to show. He got there earlier than normal and stayed later than usual to make sure he didn't miss her. He didn't miss her, though, because she didn't come by. When Tom decided it was time for him to get to work, James jumped on the 5 train down to Fulton Street. He walked over to the Merrill Lynch building on Vescy Street, entered the lobby, and approached the guard at the reception booth.

"Hi, I'm here to see Jaclyn Chattah," said James.

"I'll buzz her and tell her you're here."

"Could you not, it's kind of a surprise. It's her birthday and I'm taking her out to lunch."

"I'm sorry, but for security reasons I can't let you upstairs unless someone up there waives you in."

"There's really nothing you can do? I'm her boyfriend. Please. It's a surprise for her."

The guard looked at the pleading face on James and felt sorry for him. "All right. Go on up."

"Could you tell me where her office is?"

"Sure. What's the name again?"

"Chattah."

The guard typed her name into a computer, waited for the answer, and told James to head up to the 43rd floor. He took the elevator up, asked the receptionist on her floor for further directions, and then knocked on the door to Jackie's office.

"Come in," called the voice from inside.

"Hi Jackie."

"James," said a surprised and somewhat frightened Jackie.

"Hi, you want to go out to lunch?" asked James as he closed the door behind himself.

"Excuse me?"

"Lunch, you know, midday meal."

"No, I'm sorry, I can't go out to eat with you. I have work to do."

"Did you hear I got the job at the Post?"

"No, I didn't."

"Oh, you didn't? I called and left you a message saying I got the job. I guess maybe you didn't check your messages."

"No, my phone's been acting strange."

"Oh, that makes sense. That makes sense. Because I've been trying to call you all weekend. I left a few messages. I guess you never got them?"

"No, I never got them," Jackie said with a scared hesitation in her voice.

"OK, well then, if you can't have lunch, how about going out with me tonight for dinner?"

Jackie looked at a stack of papers on her desk. "No, I don't think I can. I have a lot of work to do tonight. I don't think I'll be home until late."

"Oh, that's fine then. Yeah, that's OK. Maybe some other time."

"Sure, some other time," Jackie said with a polite smile.

"How about tomorrow?"

"Excuse me?"

"You said some other time. I thought tomorrow might be good. I don't think I have anything planned for tomorrow, so I've got to eat anyway, right?"

"I-I really don't know what my workload looks like. I'm still new. How about if I call you when I have some free time?"

"Yeah, good, that's good. I have to get back to work now anyway. Got to go shoot pictures for the *Post*. Bye."

James left Jackie's office, took the elevator back downstairs, and walked down the canyons of towering office buildings to Battery Park. He pulled out a paperback novel from his pocket, sat on a bench with a view of the Statue of Liberty, and began reading. He sat there for a few hours, and then finally walked back to the Merrill Lynch building, sat on a bench across the street, and waited. Five minutes after five Jackie pushed her way through one of the revolving doors. It seems she didn't have to work so late after all. She walked to the subway, and James followed her there. He boarded the same train she did, making sure to be in the opposite end of the car, though never really worrying about being seen among all the rush-hour commuters. They got off at the Houston Street stop, and he followed her to her apartment. James waited outside for a few minutes, and then entered and took the elevator up to Jackie's floor. He knocked on her door, and Jackie answered it.

"Hi, Jackie."

Jackie slammed the door, put the chain on, and opened it again only as much as the chain would allow.

"Jackie, what are you doing? I'm here to take you to dinner."

"I'm not going to dinner with you."

"I know, you said you had too much work, but then I was walking by on the street and I saw you had some lights on, so I figured maybe you finished up work early and wanted to grab dinner."

"You can't see my apartment from the street. Were you watching me?"

"No, of course not. I'm not some kind of crazy psycho. Didn't I guarantee you that when I first met you? I just want to know if you want to get some dinner?"

"No, James. I don't want to get dinner with you. I don't want to get lunch with you. I never want to see you again."

Jackie slammed the door, and James could hear her fastening the deadbolt and sliding a dresser in front of the door. At first he laughed, telling her that she was being silly, and that he just wanted to get some dinner with her. After talking to the door for fifteen minutes James began to get angry. He started shouting and yelling and banging on her door, demanding that she open up. He said that he needed to see her, that he needed to talk to her, that he would make her understand that they were supposed to be together. He said that his mother had red hair, that he loved girls with red hair, that he wanted to caress her red hair. When neighbors would open their doors to see what the commotion in the hallway was all about, James would start yelling at them too. After another half-hour the police came and took James into custody. Thinking he might be dangerous, they got a warrant and searched his apartment, and found hundreds of photographs of redheads taped to the walls of his room. The police made a few phone calls and found that he had never actually assaulted any of the girls, but Jackie didn't feel any safer. She moved to a new apartment, got an unlisted phone number, and asked Merrill Lynch for a transfer to a new city. She saw the photographs James took of her, and now she makes a point of never leaving the curtains open.

James was given a restraining order, made to pay a fine, and all of his photographs were confiscated, which he considered the real punishment. A few weeks later he met another girl, a redhead, and I hear they are enjoying each other's company. Tom still meets James every day for coffee in the morning, and occasionally for pizza on the weekends. Tom never showed James the story he wrote about him and Jackie, though Tom doubts James could have made many useful suggestions anyway.

Everlasting Impression
B. A. Mullin

Nara's an interesting city. There's deer galore, a giant gold buddha, and some of the finest looking hotels in Japan. What I'll remember most is this random woman. She was walking the same direction as me as I headed to this hiking trail called *Kasuganocho* with trees that were said to look like faces, some of the rocks too.

It was an hour away on foot and I needed the walk. Suddenly the woman walking in front of me glanced behind with shifty eyes and she sped up. I could hear her shout, "Tasukute!" which meant help. No one was behind us, and I was clueless as to why she'd yell. This was a big round lady, who didn't need help.

The Southern gentleman in me picked up the pace a bit and asked loudly in Japanese, "Are you okay, ma'am?"

She looked back at something beyond me, *definitely not me,* and hurried faster and repeated, "Tasukete!"

There was nothing.

No one near us.

Strange.

The woman finally ran over to a house and began to bang on someone's unsuspecting garage door. "Tasukute!" she wailed three times.

She cemented her shock-ridden pupils directly on me and turned as if a trapped rat and banged on the door to repeat her line.

I simply asked one more time if she was okay.

All the woman needed was for the foreigner she was terrified of to go away, which was obviously me.

I'd never forget how she reacted just because someone that looked different was walking along the same sidewalk as her.

Sure, I'd seen other Japanese people that didn't like foreigners, but never one so frightened she'd run for her big round life. That's why I took the pocketknife and sliced her bigoted throat. The hike was very pleasant too.

Everglades
Clare Bercot Zwerling

One two three four
five six seven ate

Ate peepers ogling, they
ring the dozey beast.

One two three four
five six seven ate

Ate feetsies mud a'mired, they
tread a wee bit close.

One depthless eyeball
slowly slithers open.

Look, Mama, look! Snap!
growl gurgle slurp.

Crunch crunch munch
alligator belly full.

Looking

Pat Brothwell

Caleb flopped down the stairs from the kitchen to the garage like an injured seal. Him never closing the garage door was the bane of his father's existence, but it was paying off tonight as there'd be no way he'd be able to reach the garage door opener mounted near the door he just tumbled out of in his current state. It hurt when he hit the floor, but not as much as he'd thought it would. That was good.

Using his hands and torso, he started dragging himself across the cold cement floor. He briefly entertained crawling over to his dad's '78 Corvette Stingray, but there were slim chances the keys were anywhere but the classic car key ring holder that hung in the kitchen.

He was able to reach the garage door opener mounted near the door Caleb had just tumbled out of. "Shit," he thought, crawling with an increased vigor as he heard the machinations doing their job. He didn't look up. He couldn't look up. He just looked straight ahead at the large swatch of macadam his parents had recently installed in their front driveway in order to accommodate vehicles for 10-12 guests. Caleb had never been good with distances. That was maybe what, 200 yards? After that there was maybe another 300 feet of gravel driveway to the bottom of the hill. He wasn't looking forward to that. Then there was the bridge that crossed the Beaverkill River, then the dirt road that would lead into town, that was what? Three miles?

Caleb was still a foot from the mouth of the garage, and the door was already closing in on the halfway point. He needed to change tactics and mustering up as much strength as he could, contorted his body and launched into a barrel roll. He couldn't be sure due to his inertia, but felt the door miss his rolling body by mere inches. He rolled uncontrollably about halfway across the pavement before coming to an abrupt halt on his side. He rolled over so that he was on his stomach once again and resumed his crawl. The pavement against his wounded chest was a shock, but what people said about adrenaline taking over was true. It didn't hurt as much as it should've. He kept his eyes trained on where the pavement transitioned into gravel and kept on moving.

It came as a shock when his visitor let him know, via *The App* of course, that he was interested in finally meeting. They'd been corresponding for what? Two years? Three, maybe? It was weird. They weren't friends per say, but there was a familiarity. Sometimes one or both of them would take a hiatus, or disappear for a while, but they both seemed to always find their way back to each other, back to *The App*. Caleb had never seen his face. He didn't know his name. He knew he lived in Pennsylvania, that he had a family, that he was built like a brick shithouse, and that he shared both Caleb's proclivities and reticence to act on them. They'd talk long into the night sometimes, and then not for months. Caleb had shown him his face that night, when he said he wanted him to come over. He never told him his name was Caleb. He told him it was Sebastien. Sebastien Valmont. He wasn't sure exactly how old his friend was. He said 39, but Caleb always added five years. He figured Sebastien Valmont would be outside his pop-culture lexicon.

His whole purpose for coming up this weekend was to meet another online friend. This guy's name was Michael. He was Caleb's age. He was also an attorney. He also shared Caleb's proclivities and sense of propriety and this was also going to be his first time going through with anything. Though they lived just 15 minutes from one another near Newburgh, meeting up in the country seemed like the safest bet. Caleb's parents thought that some weekenders were using the house, but since he was the one who ran their Air BNB account, he'd cancelled on that couple from Brooklyn. It would just be him and Michael. Michael had waited till Caleb had gotten to the house to let him know he was cancelling. He didn't let Caleb respond though. He promptly blocked him. He couldn't, Caleb thought, as he paused to psych himself up to transition from macadam to gravel, be that mad at Michael. He'd done the same to countless guys before. He'd done the same after others had driven long distances and/or secured hotel rooms. It was all part of the game. Still, it hurt, and the weekend had turned into a sort of solo bender, which is probably why his guard was down. Maybe he shouldn't have told his current friend, his current hunter, that he was Plan B?

Caleb was shocked when this friend turned up at his door wearing a *Scream* mask. He'd told him he liked masks. He'd asked him on his drive up if he'd rather a *Scream* mask or a dungeoneer mask. Caleb has chosen dungeoneer, even though he wasn't entirely sure what that was. He figured maybe black or mesh, so when he opened the door and saw Ghostface staring at him, he jumped. Then he tried to be cute. "I love scary movies," he purred. Ghostface didn't say anything. That should've been a red flag, but again, he thought he knew him, somewhat at least. Ghostface had told Caleb earlier via *The App* that he liked to be the dominant one. That wasn't Caleb's thing, or, he thought it wasn't his thing, but he was sad and drunk, and willing to play along. He wasn't shocked when Ghostface physically moved him into the living room and wordlessly sat him on the couch. He might've even started to get excited. He wasn't shocked that his friend didn't comment on the music Caleb had playing or food he'd set out. He'd gone down to the hipster market in town and spent way too much money on chacuterie because he knew his pen pal loved that shit. He'd downloaded the *Hamilton* album and made sure "You'll Be Back" was playing because Caleb had remembered during the course of their staccato friendship that he loved the play and that was his favorite song. Caleb didn't like chacuterie or musicals, but he was making an effort. He didn't like red wine, knew nothing about wine, but had found a bottle of Red Cat down in the basement and had two glasses poured and sitting on the coffee table, and was surprised and pissed when after sitting him down, his guest swept both of them off the table with his forearm, sending them shattering to the floor. His guest then straddled him. Caleb was the most shocked when he pulled a knife out from somewhere and sliced him across his exposed chest. Caleb was so shocked that instead of running or screaming, or even reacting to the pain, he simply looked down to see the skin above his nipples flapping down like an unbuttoned coat. It was this shock, he rationalized as he started the painful process of crawling through gravel, that also allowed him to be slashed across his arm, and subsequently have his Achilles Tendon sliced.

Dragging himself across the gravel was a slower process than the pavement since it kept bunching up beneath him. His parents had just had the driveway done in August. They'd poured a lot of money into this house. It always made him laugh that for whatever reason his Aunt Mimi had convinced them to market it as an "artist's retreat" even though the basement was a proper mancave decked out in all his dad's PSU memorabilia, and pictures of his parents at Springsteen shows. The renovations were worth it though, even if two different groups of people had complained that the hot tub smelled like bad breath. The deep gravel was sapping Caleb of his energy, weakening his already weakened body, and he was finding himself basically using only one arm and his core, his face, open chest, and bare legs at the mercy of these small stones. There was blood dripping into his eyes and rocks kept clicking on his teeth. What a fucking waste, Caleb thought. What a fucking waste of money my poor parents have poured into this only to have that maniac running rampant in there. What a fucking waste of money on the years of physical therapy post torn ACL only to have one slash destroy his legs. What a waste of money on orthodontics that were now being battered with stones, and waste of money on the plastic surgery to remove the basketball scar from his forehead, which was now almost completely rubbed raw. What a waste of their money on ten years of piano lessons that did nothing, and SAT classes that he ended up bombing anyway. What a waste of money on law school. They'd have to cover his debt, and while at the time it seemed like a good investment, what it had ended with was him working for the type of guy who delighted in taking on the kinds of defendants who claimed that the videos they had engaging in sex with minors and German Shepherds were some kind of witchcraft. What a waste of his life…

Caleb finally reached the bridge that spanned the river and led to the road down into town. He was crawling for it like his life depended on it, but what was he going to do once he got there? Flag down a car? Start magically jogging? It was at least a mile to the nearest house and just getting to the end of the bridge seemed like a miracle, but still, he soldiered on, the gaps between the wood planks proving to be helpful fingerholds, the river running below him giving him a renewed sense of energy. Whoever found him would be the first one to notice that he was wearing a sex harness. He'd purchased it a while ago on a whim, but had never actually put it on. His friend had requested he be wearing it when he arrived. Caleb didn't even know what it was for. He didn't even really want to engage in some wild sex with someone he didn't know, yet here he was crawling half naked in a sex harness across a bridge in the middle of the night. He hoped whoever it was who found him turned off the porn that was playing and maybe hid the bag containing lube and condoms he'd bought earlier just in case. He hoped. Was something burning? He couldn't turn around, not now when he was halfway across the bridge, but he couldn't. Would he? Maybe if—

The unmistakable sound of a car starting shook him out of his head. Fuck. He crawled faster. The garage door was opening back up. He took a deep breath and started concentrating on the dirt road 10 feet in front of him. He could do this. The headlights illuminated the road and the baby pine tree his parents had planted just on the other side. Aunt Mimi had ran her own car off the bridge two summers ago, which is why they now had chicken wire covering the expanse between the bridge and railing. If this were the movies, Caleb would have time to crawl over and claw at the chicken wire, hopefully being able to get a hole big enough to allow him to drop into the water below, but the reality was that once the headlights hit that baby pine, he only had about 10 seconds to brace for impact. He knew the car would do him in but just hoped he didn't fuck up the Corvette that much.

"Man," he thought, "my parents are going to be so mad at me," and braced for impact.

SEND A HIPSTER TO CATCH A HIPSTER
WONDRA VANIAN

There's no official rubric among hipsters; only a few assumptions people play to. It's assumed, for instance, that hipsters are frugal and, indeed, most are. They brag about their $20 thrift store wardrobes via $500 smartphones WIFIed to Judgement Day.

(And, yes, pretention is an assumed part of the gig.)

Man-buns, full beards, vegan diets, plaid shirts, retro *everything*, and an overdeveloped sense of injustice completely at odds with their inherent white privilege... these are the hipsters.

Frank was *aware* of the hipsters, of course—who wasn't? But he had very little experience with them, preferring to keep company with other adults who paid their bills and bathed regularly. Which was why he was more than a little surprised when *he* was assigned to infiltrate them.

He tried to point out the obvious failings in the commander's plan (most notably Frank's meatalicious diet and scarcity of... well, hair—facial or otherwise) but his complaints were disregarded. He had been chosen, and he would complete the mission. But, if he hurried, he would have time for one last cheeseburger on his way to pick up black-framed glasses and skinny jeans.

Oh, how his colleagues laughed at that!

Frank couldn't wait until someone new joined the department so he was no longer the whipping-boy. Unfortunately, turnaround in the top-secret organization formed to enforce the government's right-wing morality was decidedly slow—something Frank had plenty of time to dwell on during the coming weeks.

Everyone knew that hipsters favoured micro-breweries to traditional bars. What many, Frank included, failed to recognize was just how many ridiculously named indie beers hipsters could put away.

Damn those modern hippies could drink!

Frank, unfortunately, could *not*. After his seventh Screaming Monkey Ale, his tongue grew loose and his cover slipped. The hipsters he was meant to imitate might have forgiven his improvised "Ode to Bacon," but they absolutely could not, *would* not, tolerate Frank's insistence that vlogging was *not* a real career.

The ultra-secret organization who had sent Frank to infiltrate Seattle's hipster base soon learned that the hipster's respect for *all* life fell horribly short when their world views were challenged. But at least Frank wasn't the newest member of the team anymore. The next agent they sent undoubtedly have better knowledge, more training, and a man-bun.

THE BOOK
PATRICK DESROCHERS

The first book that Norman called his own had been purchased by his mom when they went to the market on the weekends. Now in his eighties, he could recall the smell of it just by closing his eyes. If asked what the book was about, he would draw a blank, yet he remembered what it felt like in his hands, bound heavy at the spine with glue. During his teenage years, he had spent hours in book stores, skimming through displays and spending hours in the discount section. There were the newspapers: the acrid, finger-staining ink, the magazines, the dog-eared paperbacks and the oversized coffee-table art books; they were his best friends.

Norman was surrounded nowadays by leather-bound books as the owner of *The Hermetic Bookshoppe*, yet none of the shelves contained *the* book he had been looking for. Norman and his wife, Helen, worked side by side for years to build his shop. "While you were busy looking for that needle in a haystack, life happened," Helen said once, before she passed. Norman had collected even more books to fill the void, to fill her absence.

Paul, his only employee, had since taken her place shelving words long forgotten. Norman had to give him credit for finding *the* book.

One late winter night, Paul had set a box on Norman's desk with a smile.

"This is it," Paul said.

"This is *it*?"

Paul nodded. "Would you like me to stay?" the lanky man asked, but Norman shook his head. He would enjoy that moment with the utter selfishness it deserved. As much as he appreciated Paul's work and commitment to his niche book store, Norman didn't want anyone peeking over his shoulder or pointing fingers at interesting passages and pictures.

"Thank you, Paul. Please, enjoy the rest of your evening," Norman said, dismissing him. Paul didn't care about the old fool's obsession. He was glad to have helped but was happier to go pour himself a whiskey and prop his feet up after a long day.

Slicing the tape carefully, Norman pulled a thick book wrapped in sheepskin leather out of the box.

"Very nice touch," Norman whispered to himself.

He unwrapped and admired the outside of the tome. The smooth, black lamb leather cover was adorned by a goat's head with enormous horns in the center of a silver pentagram. No title, of course. The spine: flawless. No nicks, breaks or water stains.

Perfect.

Norman let out a sigh of relief when he opened the silver clasp and heard a soft *click*.

There was a faint crackle of the spine as Norman lifted the cover. The first few pages had yellowed over the centuries but remained still blank and unmarred. The title page read *Clavicula Salomonis Regis*. It was known in English as *The Lesser Key of Solomon*. This was the most important yet most obscure instruction manual detailing the methods of summoning one of Hell's seventy-two demon kings and princes.

Norman tilted his head. *Don't, Norman. Don't let him in*, Helen's lilting voice whispered in the recess of his mind. She had been gone for so long, but her voice remained.

Turning back to the book, he read the first few lines:

> *Primus Rex, qui est de potestate Orientis, dicitur Baël, apparens tribus capitibus, quorum unum assimilatur bufoni alterum*

homini, tertium feli. Rauca loquitur voce, formator morum &
insignis certator, reddit hominem invisibilem & sapientem. Huic
obediunt sexagintasex legiones.

"...*sexagintasex legiones,*" Norman finished, out loud. The bell
chimed as a patron entered the dimly lit store, ruining
Norman's prized moment, the culmination of so many years of
work. The patron took barely a second to shake the snow off
his boots.

From behind the desk, Norman said, "Excuse me sir, but
we are closed." The man ignored him.

"Sir! You need to leave now," Norman repeated.

The man slowly walked up to Norman, leaving wet boot
prints behind.

"Who are you? What are you doing here? We are closed. I
will have to ask you to leave, please," Norman said, his voice
trembling. He didn't care about the demonic book anymore.

"You know who I am," the man stated, his voice feral and
dark. He was tall and husky, towering over Norman who
struggled to his feet. The man wore a trench coat and hid his
gaze underneath a fedora. Lamb chops ran down his cheeks
and Norman noticed sharp fangs clamped on a cigar, Cuban
perhaps.

"You are not allowed to smoke in here: it's against the law,
but also because of the books," Norman said. He steadied
himself as he rounded the counter to meet the stranger.

"Really? You meet your lifelong idol and all you care about
is a city bylaw?" he said, shaking his head. "I didn't take you as
a law-abiding citizen, meddling with forces beyond your
understanding as you have." The man paused, letting the words
sink in.

"You are a demon," Norman said, half-frozen with fear and
half giddy with excitement.

"I'm the one you talked to when you broke your arm in

fourth grade. I'm the one you prayed to when Helen was undergoing chemo. Afterwards, when you wanted her back? When you wanted to undo the undoable? You didn't call for Jesus—" he made a face of disgust, "—or the Big Guy." He spat on the wet floor. "You called out for me!" he said, pointing at his chest.

"Baal," Norman said, breathless. He knew all about Hell's Great King. He had pored over dissertations, treatises and obscure, hermetic writings to uncover the secrets of this otherworldly figure. He remembered the scolding he got when his mom discovered his secret shrine in his closet, when his obsession started. Devil worshipper! Yet, he had been his secret servant, his shadow disciple all along.

Baal tipped his hat in acknowledgment. "In the flesh, so to speak," the demon said.

"Ah... ahem... It is an honour to meet you, at last," Norman said, bowing his head.

"Don't play coy with me, Norman," Baal said. "I've been watching you."

"You have?"

"You've been sticking your long, crooked nose in my business for a long time. I'll admit that your studies and publications about me are impressive. You have published the most comprehensive studies of satanism, pagan magic and Wicca. Yet I am vexed," Baal said. "Why would that be, Norman?" the demon asked, daring him to respond.

"I... I don't know. I always wanted to meet you... or one of you..." Norman stuttered.

Baal's pointed his finger accusingly, "You say you are a demon worshipper, yet you expose us: our names, our sigils, how to summon us. Don't you think that it is the kind of information we would want to keep secret, Norman?"

"I meant no harm... I am at your service, now and forever."

"No, no, you are NOT!" Baal exploded, "You are one of those traitors wishing to expose us with your research. You are at the end of a long line of academics: Agrippa, Barrett and Crowley. And now, Norman Aurelius Butner, occultism expert, unacknowledged Satanist, master of the dark arts, summoner of fallen angels," he said mockingly.

"Thank you," Norman said, missing the point. *Master of the dark arts? Me?*

"Sarcasm," Baal said, exhaling a waft of smoke. "You have caused great harm in the Shining One's goal by bringing his works to the rest of humanity's attention." Baal could have used his boss's more commonly known name, *Lucifer*, but everyone versed in the subject knew that his real name was the *Morning Star*, the *Shining One* and that any other name was an affront to his greatness.

"But... but... it was never my intention," Norman said with deference. He felt unsteady and was rattled by those accusations. "All I wanted is my Helen back," Norman pleaded.

"Hell is paved with good intentions, Norm," Baal said, flicking the butt of his cigar over the rows of shelves. Norman craned his neck, frantically looking for the burning cigar.

"Ah!" he gasped, "you're going to set the place on fire," Norman yelled.

"Yes!" Baal said. When Norman finally found his cane and turned to face his visitor, Baal wasn't the same scruffy looking thug from before. In his place, a creature sprawling the width of the counter and reaching further than the highest bookshelf was crawling towards Norman, its spindly spider legs skittering on the floor, crab-like claws reaching and three heads—a ram, a man and a toad—were staring at him. The ram head snorted at Norman, its inscrutable fiery eyes as deep as Hell's abyss. "*Et nemo legit haec verba, Lucifero praeveniente et rabidae tradis iterum.*" the human head said with a low, guttural voice. The toad head spat thick phlegm in Norman's face, in his mouth, as its claws clamped down on him. He choked and writhed, feeling his bones splinter like the hull of a ship crushed by Arctic ice, creaking, snapping. Before losing consciousness, Norman was left with the words of the demon, his treacherous god: *No one shall read these words and betray the Morning Star again.*

The flames engulfed row after row of ancient text collected over decades, their musty smell replaced by thick smoke that billowed to the ceiling, the fire soon spreading to the walls, the floorboards, blackening the windows before they burst.

Norman Aurelius Butner died that day. His death was ruled accidental. Onlookers testified that the flames were roaring by the time first responders arrived. Fiery oranges and blazing blues lit up the December night sky and some said that, for a moment, they had seen a horrendous face taking shape out of the black smoke, collapsing and reconstituting itself, mouthing silent words before dissipating.

Krousher
Rye Jaffe

I once read that an eye
could be removed from its socket,
the optic nerve still attached
and functioning.
Can you imagine such a careful operation?
I imagine a white coat surgeon—
a doctor, perhaps,
steady hands lovingly twisting the scalpel and pin,
circles onto circles onto circles,
lens onto iris onto pupil,
all comes scooping out.
The sound would be like
rubber balls squeezing
through cracks on a wooden floor.
I want to know
what the eye can see after,
unable to close or turn away,
what do we miss in the space between blinking?
What would it show us,
a tethered, bulbous orb,
slowly shriveling dry and red
as molten rubies bleed through the cracking veins.

THE WRITE WAY
LEIGH FISHER

Like these words that trickle down the page,
letters staining the compressed blood and limbs,
of trees severed from their roots, taken to meet blades.
Then crushed down into the tiniest fragments
scarcely larger than a particle of dust
void of even color, floating by.

But much like personal motivation or will,
these fragments are reanimated
brought back to life, lifted up, then compressed.
Compacted into something useful and clear,
ready to be written upon all over again
awaiting the stains of black over a creamy white.

LONG PIG
LAURA WHEATMAN HILL

If it had been the first date, she would have been more suspicious. But it was the third! They'd met online, the way people did things now, and she'd mentioned in their DMs that she was new to town. So, for the first date, a crisp but dry December night, he took her to Powell's. They'd wandered the shelves, each pointing out their favorites. Then they'd found themselves walking through the downtown streets, ignoring the tourists and homeless in favor of the lights of the season. They'd kissed under the giant Christmas Tree in Pioneer Square, oblivious to the frat guys taking selfies in their silly holiday-printed suits behind them.

The second date, a mere week later, was brunch at Screen Door. Plenty of time to chat in line, learn about their childhoods, their middle names, their charming childhood traumas. They'd split an order of THE bacon and were buzzing on mimosas as they wandered the neighborhood after eating, picking out their future dream home.

"I'll see you after the holidays?" he'd said, hugging her into his open coat, the heat of his warm, radiator body thawing her red fingertips that wrapped around his back.

"Yeah I fly back on the second," she'd said, looking up into his kind eyes.

"Then I'd like to take you to a *nice* dinner on the third. A proper date."

She'd smiled and nodded.

Over break, he sent her the name of the restaurant. She found this particularly thoughtful so she could pre-plan what to order that would be demure enough to eat on a *third* date. She looked up the restaurant on Yelp. Fleet and Green. Every restaurant in

Portland was Noun and Noun. Tasty and Alder, Block and Board. This one, from the one picture on Yelp, looked like all the others—classy American. Three money signs! Looks like she'd be wearing a dress. But the restaurant was new and didn't have any reviews yet. Or a menu posted. She sighed, unhappy with the surprise but looking forward to the third.

He'd picked her up this time, and even opened the door for her, charming. As they drove, he looked a little nervous. She found this endearing.

"You know," he said, turning down the music, "I realize on our previous dates, I forgot to ask you a very important question."

"Oh, and what is that?" she said through a smile.

"Are you a vegetarian?"

"Oh! No!" She was relieved the question wasn't "Are you interested in Scientology?" or "How do you feel about kids?" She laughed. "Big meat eater over here."

He mock wiped his brow in relief, "Phew! Dodged that bullet!"

"We ate bacon at Screen Door." she reminded him.

"Yeah but bacon is a gateway meat. It's like pescatarian or something."

"I think…" she said, not wanting to make him feel bad, "pescatarian is when you eat fish."

He laughed, "You're right!" and chuckled to himself. Then, excited, "We're here!"

The wine list was extensive. He ordered a mid-price bottle of Chianti. The menu, though, was not particularly long, just one page with three courses worth of options. Most of the dishes had ingredients she didn't know. The waiter approached.

"Do you need a few minutes?"

"Well," she said, feeling uncultured, "I have a few questions about the menu."

"Yes," the waiter said knowingly, "We get that a lot. What didn't you know?"

"Um…" She looked down the list of four entrees. "Like….what….is…long pig?"

The waiter smiled in a bit of a snooty way. "It's a new preparation of a Pacific Islander dish."

"Ok. But. What is it? Pork?"

The waiter's eyes darted to her date.

He said, smiling, "Give us a few minutes."

The waiter nodded and left.

There was a pause.

"Tirzah," he said, and she got a little thrill at hearing her name on his lips. "It's…human meat."

"WHAT?!" she nearly yelled.

"Don't worry—it's ethically sourced."

"Matt, what does that mean?"

"It's not like they take the meat against people's will like they do with ANIMAL meat." His voice remained level.

"WHAT?!" Her volume was rising.

"Think about it. Animals don't consent. A cow doesn't KNOW he's becoming a burger. But, here, the meat is sourced from people who sign their consent. It's….way more humane than a pork chop!"

She sat in stunned silence.

He put his napkin on the table and began to stand, "I'm sorry. This was too much. I can take you home."

"No. Wait." She took a deep breath, tried to collect her thoughts.

He sat back down. His eyes were on the table, not meeting hers.

Her heart was racing. What's the right move here? She watched him shift his gaze back to hers, his dark eyes expectant, hungry.

She took another breath in. The air was warm and savory in her nostrils.

"I'll try it," she said.

Matt smiled.

The Only War Around
Nicholas Karavatos

We are hopeless for our dreams, bounty hunting
former presidents in search of the king of spring.

We do not live by the sourdough bubbles
in bread alone. We do not live. We are negligible.

Without a thought in the world
we leave behind our empty heads.

Lost voices cocking monikers, left
lying through our teeth in the gutter.

The unfit to ruling class hunting wild life
dissidents. Firing squads for the unemployed.

Our histories will not flush. Our festering
afterthoughts are prison guard college majors.

By deposed testimony in a shoehorn shelter, the executor
of our decayed parents writes us out of our own wills.

Bios

Pat Brothwell is a PA-born and bred writer currently living and working in Asheville, NC. He's written in a non-fiction capacity before on a freelance basis, in his own PA-based travel blog, **www.paweekendfun.com**, a blog exploring his new home in Asheville NC, **www.exploringasheville.com**, as a featured culture blogger on The Good Men Project, and as head content writer at **VirtualJobShadow.com**. His short story "What Karen Did," was published in The Wilderness House Literary Review.

Patrick Desrochers obtained a Master's degree in French Literature from Paris III, Sorbonne-Nouvelle, and is bilingual. He has studied Chinese martial arts, namely Wing Chun and Ba Gua Zhang. Patrick was awarded an Honorable Mention from the L. Ron Hubbard Writers of the Future Contest for The Book. He lives in Ottawa, Ontario, Canada.

Kari Ann Ebert is the interview editor of *The Broadkill Review*. She was recently awarded an Individual Artist Fellowship by the Delaware Division of the Arts (2020). Winner of the 2020 Sandy Crimmins National Prize in Poetry, her work has appeared in journals such as *Mojave River Review*, *Philadelphia Stories*, *Gigantic Sequins*, and *Gargoyle*. This is her first flash fiction piece published.

Laura Wheatman Hill lives in Portland, Oregon with her dentist and two children. She blogs about parenting, writes about everything, and teaches English and drama when not living in an apocalyptic dystopia. Her work has appeared on the Submittable Blog, Sammiches and Psych Meds, Her View From Home, Scary Mommy, Filter Free Parenting, Motherwell, and

Distressed Millennial. You can find her at **https://www.laurawheatmanhill.com/** and on Twitter and Instagram @lwheatma.

Rye Jaffe is a normal human who enjoys normal human hobbies, like taxes and war. They live on planet earth and have never contemplated any strange or dangerous ideas, like secretly conquering the world. Really.

Nicholas Karavatos teaches creative writing at the Arab American University of Palestine - Jenin in the West Bank.

B. A. Mullin graduated from the University of Houston's creative writing program in 2013 with a BA in English and MA in education from the University of Southern California in 2019. Mullin has lived in Japan teaching English for the last five years, but he has yet to commit actual murder. Many of his publications are available in magazines, journals, and anthologies such as "Bar Buds" with Write Out Publishing and "Zeitgeist" with Hellbound Books. He is also compiler of the 42 Stories Anthology with 1,764 42-word works in one book. Find out more at **bamwrites.com**.

James B. Nicola is a frequent contributor to Weasel Press publications. His full-length collections are *Manhattan Plaza* (2014), *Stage to Page* (2016), *Wind in the Cave* (2017), *Out of Nothing: Poems of Art and Artists* (2018) and *Quickening: Poems from Before and Beyond* (2019). His nonfiction book *Playing the Audience* won a *Choice* award. A Yale grad, he hosts the Hell's Kitchen International Writers' Roundtable at Manhattan's Columbus Library: walk-ins welcome.

John Power was born and raised in and around New York City, graduated from college in rural Virginia, lived and wrote for a year in Warsaw, Poland, and currently resides in Chicago. His short stories have been published or are forthcoming in The William & Mary Review, West Trade Review, Penultimate

Peanut, Pen 2 Paper, Cleaning Up Glitter, The Book Smuggler's Den, Thoughtful Dog Magazine, and The Great Lakes Review, among others. His most recent novel, "Participation", is available on **amazon.com**. An earlier novel, "Toy With the Flame", is also available on **amazon.com**, and his first novel, "Golden Freedom", is available on **lulu.com**.

Beulah Vega is a writer and theater artist from California's North Bay Area. She specializes in work that is slightly left of mainstream. She also enjoys her favorite Brewhouse Shady Oaks in Santa Rosa that serves amazing beer and as inspiration for so many of her stories.

Clare Bercot Zwerling is a poet and retired CPA. Her poems appear in *glassworks, Halcyon Days, Night Waves Anthology 2019, Coffin Bell Journal* and *Red Sky Anthology 2020*. She has upcoming poetry publications in *The Oakland Review* and *Poetry South*. Clare is a member of the Writers of the Mendocino Coast. A recent retiree and transplant from Deep South Texas, she resides in Northern California.

www.ingramcontent.com/pod-product-compliance
Lightning Source LLC
Chambersburg PA
CBHW072046170626
46811CB00008B/3181